Dread in the Dark

Dread in the Dark

Story by *Tuula Pere*
Illustrations by *Catty Flores*
Layout by *Peter Stone*
English translation by *Mirka Pohjanrinne*
Edited in English by *Susan Korman*

ISBN 978-952-325-445-9 (Hardcover)
ISBN 978-952-325-446-6 (Softcover)
ISBN 978-952-325-447-3 (ePub)
First edition

Copyright © 2021 Wickwick Ltd

Published 2021 by Wickwick Ltd
Helsinki, Finland

Originally published in Finland by Wickwick Ltd in 2021
Finnish "Pimeän peikko", ISBN 978-952-325-448-0 (Hardcover), ISBN 978-952-325-450-3 (ePub)
English "Dread in the Dark", ISBN 978-952-325-445-9 (Hardcover), ISBN 978-952-325-447-3 (ePub)

Dread in the Dark

TUULA PERE · CATTY FLORES

Children's Books from the Heart

A lot has happened in Elliot's life recently.

He has a new baby sister, who needs care all the time. Mom and Dad are excited, and they often have family members visiting them to see the baby.

"Such cute little fingers!" everyone chirps.

Elliot tries to chime in, but nobody has time to listen. "Of course, her fingers are small, she's a baby!" he says. "My fingers were small too when I was a baby."

Before the baby was born, Elliot had gotten a room of his own. It's right next to the kitchen, a little bit farther away from Mom and Dad's bedroom than his old room.

His parents try to explain the new situation to him. "You do understand, Elliot, that the baby must sleep close to our bedroom, don't you? Mom has to feed the baby many times during the night."

Elliot has trouble sleeping in the new room. He worries that Mom and Dad won't hear him if he needs something at night.

5

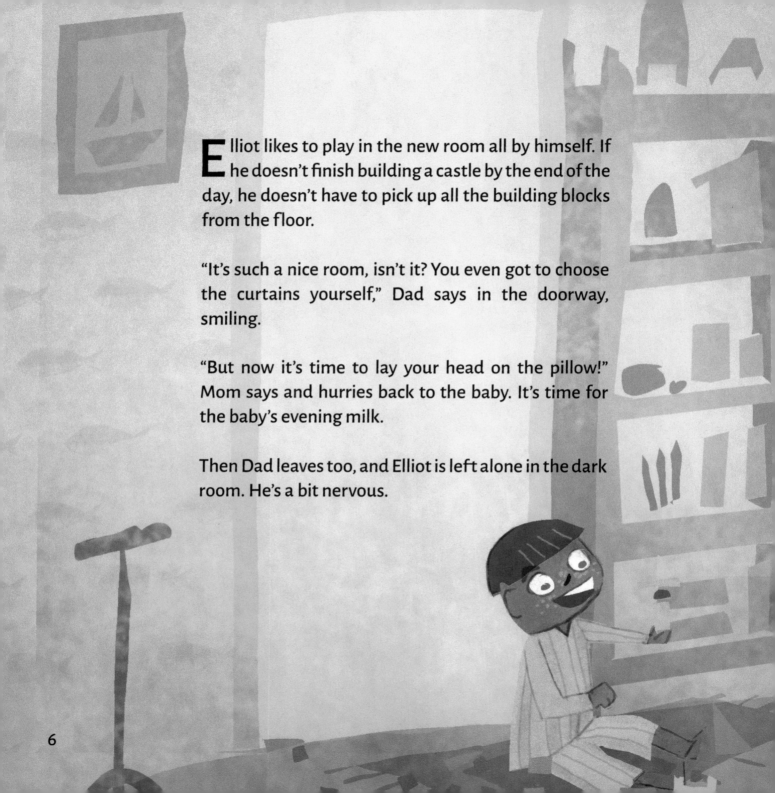

Elliot likes to play in the new room all by himself. If he doesn't finish building a castle by the end of the day, he doesn't have to pick up all the building blocks from the floor.

"It's such a nice room, isn't it? You even got to choose the curtains yourself," Dad says in the doorway, smiling.

"But now it's time to lay your head on the pillow!" Mom says and hurries back to the baby. It's time for the baby's evening milk.

Then Dad leaves too, and Elliot is left alone in the dark room. He's a bit nervous.

6

Elliot hears Dad's footsteps walk away. The room is quiet—well, almost. Elliot hears a growling sound from under the bed. *Grrowwl.* Then there is another soft noise. *Rattle, rattle!*

"I don't want to sleep in here," Elliot says quietly at first.

"I really don't want to sleep in here!" Elliot shouts, but no one answers.

"Can't anybody hear me? I want to sleep in my old room!" Elliot screams with tears in his eyes.

But the baby has started to cry so loudly, Mom and Dad can't hear Elliot's screams.

*C*lick! The light is turned off. Elliot tries to breathe silently, so Dad can hear the darkness monster. They wait, but they hear no strange sounds.

"Why don't you try to get some sleep, Elliot? I can leave the door open for you," Dad says.

Reluctantly Elliot says yes. He hugs Dad hard one more time and then slips back under his blanket.

"Good night, Dad."

Elliot is alone again. He tries to be brave. Little by little, he starts feeling more relaxed.

But then the darkness monster returns! "It's here again! Dad, come back quickly!" Elliot is terrified. *Grrowwl! Rattle, rattle!* Now the sounds are even closer!

Dad comes back and turns on the light right away.

"Listen now, Dad! The monster is under the bed," Elliot says, waving at the floor.

"Let's be quiet for a second," Dad says, trying to listen.

A steady low hum can be heard quite clearly. *Grrowwl.* Then there's a rattling sound, which grows louder before it stops.

"I think there's a very ordinary explanation for the sound," Dad says. "Why don't we go and say hello to that monster of yours together?"

"But I don't want to see it!" Elliot insists.

Dad has a sly smile. "There's nothing to be afraid of, I promise. The sounds are coming from the kitchen, and it's not a monster."

Finally Elliot dares to go with him.

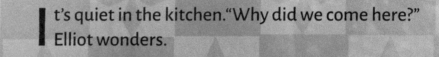

It's quiet in the kitchen. "Why did we come here?" Elliot wonders.

Dad peels an apple for both of them, and they sit down to eat them quietly.

"Now listen!" Dad says, pointing at the refrigerator.

Soon Elliot understands. The refrigerator's motor growls, and then quiets down again.

"But what about the other noise?" Elliot asks.

When Dad moves the refrigerator away from the wall, the rattle stops too.

"Thank goodness it's just a refrigerator and not a darkness monster!" Elliot says, relieved.

It's time to go back to bed. Now Elliot will sleep like a log for sure.

Elliot wants to say good night to his baby sister before going back to bed.

"Sleep peacefully, little baby! You have nothing to fear. I'm right there in the room next to you," Elliot whispers.

CPSIA information can be obtained
at www.ICGtesting.com
Printed in the USA
BVHW020731200121
598054BV00034B/414